The Easter Rooster

Written by
Daniel Williamson

Illustrated by
Kleverton Monteiro

This book is dedicated
to my daughter
Carmela

First published in 2021 by Daniel Williamson
www.danielwilliamson.co.uk
This edition published in 2021
Text © Daniel Williamson 2021
Illustrations © Kleverton Monteiro 2021
Cover design © by Uzuri Designs 2021

ISBN 978-1-913583-24-8

DW

www.danielwilliamson.co.uk

The Easter Rooster

Have you ever seen a farm at night? I mean, ever in your life?

Normally it's only seen by a farmer and his wife.

The animals all fast asleep. The moon lights up the sky.

The stars all twinkle ever so bright, when the clouds have passed on by.

When the early rays of sunlight come, someone has a job to do.

To wake up everyone on the farm, and all the animals too!

He slowly takes a great, big breath, and lets out such a sound.

'Cock-a-doodle-doo!'
He shouts, to everyone around.

He struts around the chicken coop
for security it would seem.

'Oh my, he's just so very handsome.'
'He really is a dream!'

The Rooster guards the chickens well. Right throughout the year.

But there's just one day he really hates. A day he's come to fear.

For when Easter is upon us, he goes jelly in the legs.

As every year a bunny comes and steals the chicken's eggs!

Last year he wore a chicken suit, and snuck into the coop.

The year before, he wore a tie, and brought The Rooster soup.

The year before that, he rode a cat,
and grabbed the eggs at speed.

But this
year Rooster
swore to all,
'the bunny
will not
succeed!'

The Rooster set his
bunny traps, with
a carrot in each one.

Then sat outside
the chicken coop.
Surveillance had
begun.

As the animals all went inside,
The Rooster counted the sheep.

A silly thing for him to do,
as it made him fall asleep!

Then someone crept behind The Rooster,
and left him a double surprise.

A cosy blanket over his lap,
and a mask right over his eyes.

Next day,
the chickens
woke him up.

'You forgot to Doodle-Do!
Everyone slept in today!
All because of you!'

'There's carrots on this blanket look,
it's got to be a clue.'

'I think we know what's happened here,
as our eggs have vanished too!'

The Rooster ran into the forest, he climbed the tallest tree.

But a tiny, distant, line of smoke was all that he could see.

The smoke was coming from a chimney,
on a cottage, oh so quaint.

He looked inside and saw the eggs!
But the eggs were covered in paint!

The Rooster stood aside like a gent,
to let the old lady past.

She slowly walked on to
the path, then hopped
off ever so fast!

The Rooster ran right down the path. Through the fog and haze.

At the bottom of the path he saw a green and bushy maze.

The Rooster went inside the maze.
He followed the coloured pegs,
and sure enough, he slowly found
all of the chicken's eggs!

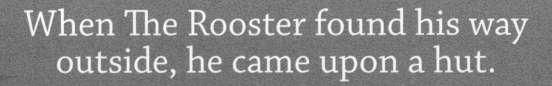

When The Rooster found his way outside, he came upon a hut.

Inside there was a big white door, with a note that said 'keep shut.'

The Rooster just could not resist,
he opened up the door.

Inside were lots of big brown eggs,
from the top, down to the floor.

'I'll take these back as well.' He said.
'Then we'll have twice as many!

I'll be the hero once again.
Adored by Jenny and Penny.'

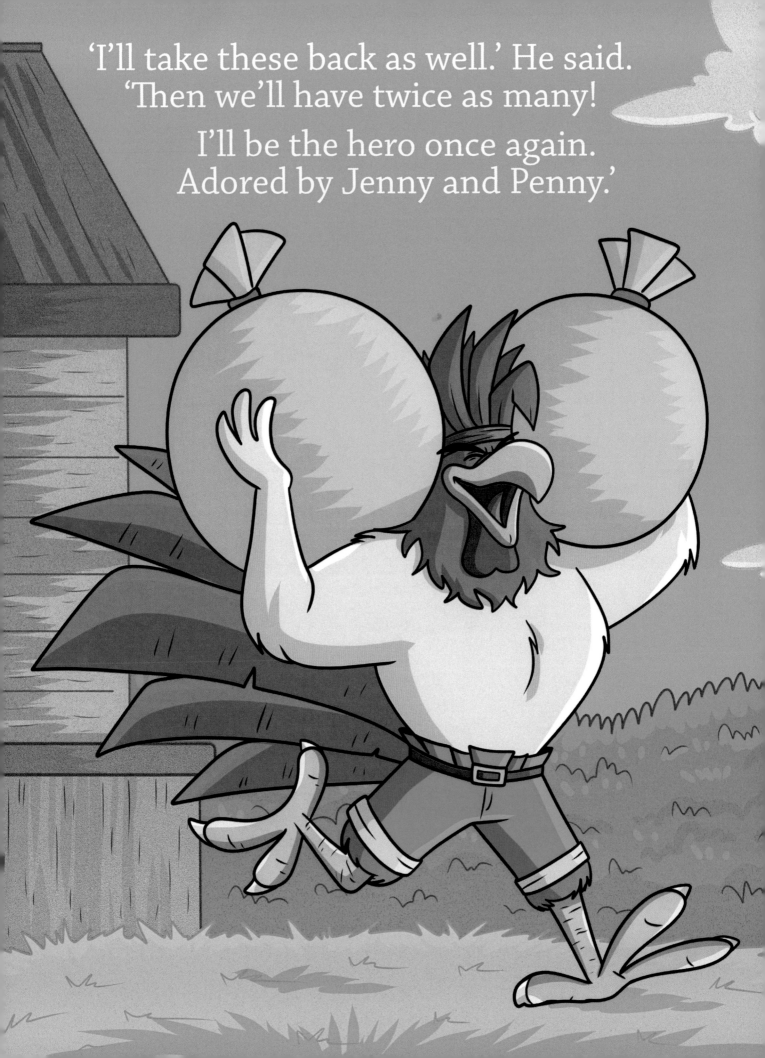

The Rooster got back to the farm.
Left the eggs out in the sun.
But little did The Rooster know,
his troubles had just begun.

The eggs were for an Easter hunt. For children on a school trip.

And when they could not find ONE egg, the children started to FLIP!

The parents tried to calm them down.
'Don't worry there's chocolate inside!'

But when they opened the big white door,
every child and grown up cried!

They all marched up on to the farm, to find who ruined their fun.

But the chocolate eggs had disappeared. All melted in the sun.

'There's chocolate on that rooster's wing!' 'Let's get him!' The children said.

The Rooster gulped, he turned around,
and off he quickly sped.
The children and the grown-ups too,
all chased The Rooster away.

As for that naughty bunny, well...

...he's still laughing to this day!

This author has developed a bilingual book series designed to introduce children to a number of new languages from a very young age.

If you enjoyed reading this story, you will undoubtedly like popular rhyming picture books from this author which are also currently available.

A Message From The Author

I'd like to say a massive thank you to every single child and adult that read one of my books! My dream is to bring cultures together through fun illustrations, imagination and creativity via the power of books.

If you would like to join me on this journey, please visit my website danielwilliamson.co.uk where each email subscriber receives a free ebook to keep or we will happily send to a friend of your choice as a gift!

Nothing makes me happier than a review on the platform you purchased my book telling me where my readers are from! Also, please click on my links below and follow me to join my ever-growing online family! Remember there is no time like the present and the present is a gift!

Yours gratefully

Daniel Williamson

@DanWAuthor

@danwauthor

@DanWAuthor